The Birthday Doll

Jane Cutler
Pictures by Hiroe Nakata

FARRAR STRAUS GIROUX · NEW YORK

For my Franny —J.C.

For my birthday dolls, who were all handmade by my mother —H.N.

Text copyright © 2004 by Jane Cutler
Illustrations copyright © 2004 by Hiroe Nakata
Distributed in Canada by Douglas & McIntyre Ltd.
Color separations by Chroma Graphics PTE Ltd.
Printed and bound in the United States by Phoenix Color Corporation
Designed by Robbin Gourley
First edition, 2004
1 3 5 7 9 10 8 6 4 2

Library of Congress Cataloging-in-Publication Data

Cutler, Jane.

    The birthday doll / Jane Cutler; pictures by Hiroe Nakata.— 1st ed.

      p. cm.

    Summary: For her birthday, Franny receives a new, fancy doll in the mail and an old rag
doll at her party, and discovers the real difference between the two.

    ISBN 0-374-30719-9

    [1. Dolls—Fiction. 2. Birthdays—Fiction. 3. Parties—Fiction.] I. Nakata, Hiroe, ill.
II. Title.

PZ7.C985Bi 2004
[E]—dc21
                                        2002044673

The doll arrived in a big box on the morning of Franny's birthday party.

"From Aunt Ida and Uncle Lou," said Franny's mom. "Do you remember them?"

Franny wasn't sure.

"The doll's name is Rose," Franny's mom told her. "See, it says so right here on the box."

"What does this say?" asked Franny, pointing to the rest of the writing.

"It says, 'Squeeze my hand and I'll talk to you!'"

Franny took Rose out of her box. Rose had plump pink cheeks and big blue eyes. She had yellow curls, and her mouth was shaped like a kiss.

Franny squeezed Rose's hand. "Ring around the rosy, pocket full of posy, ashes, ashes, we all fall down!" sang Rose.

"More!" said Franny's little brother, Ben.

Franny squeezed Rose's hand again. "Ring around the rosy, pocket full of posy, ashes, ashes, we all fall down!" sang Rose.

"More!" said Ben. He reached for Rose.

"Later," said Franny. She picked up the doll and went to her room.

Franny fluffed Rose's frilly skirt and smoothed Rose's curls. She squeezed Rose's hand again. "Ring around the rosy, pocket full of posy, ashes, ashes, we all fall down!" sang Rose.

Carefully, Franny set Rose on a chair.

Then Franny put on her party shoes and her bead necklace, combed her hair exactly the way she liked it, and went to wait for the guests.

While she was waiting, she and Ben licked the spoons and bowls their mother had used when she made the birthday cake.

They helped their father hang birthday decorations.

And when their grandmother
came with party favors and balloons,
they ran around in circles, screaming.

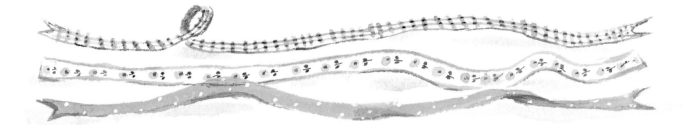

At last the guests arrived.

Franny had invited three old friends and one new one to her party.

The three old friends each brought packages wrapped in fancy paper and tied with ribbons.

The new friend brought a paper bag decorated with crayon drawings.

Franny opened the
first package. Inside
was a jigsaw puzzle
with a hundred pieces.

Franny opened the second package.
Inside was a Chinese checkers set with
a handsome wooden board.

Franny opened the third
package. Inside was a wooden
bug house with a screen.

Franny opened the paper bag. Inside
was an old rag doll with a painted face
and brown yarn hair.

"A cuddly sort of doll,"
said Grandmother, smiling and
putting it on the pile of presents.

The party was perfect.

But quick as a wink, it was over.

After the guests left, Mom gave Ben his bath.

Dad cleaned up.

Grandmother helped Franny put away her presents and get ready for bed.

Franny made room on her toy shelf for the puzzle and the Chinese checkers set and the bug house.

Grandmother held the rag doll. "Look at this, Franny," she said. "Someone has embroidered this doll's name on her underwear. Her name is Suzie."

"She's old," Franny said.

"Yes," said Grandmother.

"Her clothes are faded."

"So I see," said Grandmother.

"She's floppy," grumbled Franny.

"Her stuffing's gone flat," explained Grandmother.

"She's not pretty," Franny pointed out.

Grandmother squinted at the doll. "Not pretty," she agreed. "But her face is pleasant."

"I guess," said Franny.

Grandmother put Suzie on top of the toy shelf. The doll flopped right over.

Then Grandmother read Franny a story and tucked her in.

"I want to sleep with my birthday doll," said Franny. She pointed to Rose. "Listen, Grandmother." She squeezed Rose's hand. "Ring around the rosy, pocket full of posy, ashes, ashes, we all fall down!" Rose sang.

"Mmm," said Grandmother. She gave Franny a hug and a kiss. "Goodnight, Franny," she said. "Happy birthday."

Franny held Rose in her arms. The doll's frilly dress scratched. Her yellow curls smelled like plastic.

Franny squeezed Rose's hand and quickly let go. "Ring around the rosy..." sang Rose.

Franny squeezed and let go more quickly. "Ring around the..."

More quickly. "Ring around..."

Much more quickly. "Ring..."

Again. "Ring..."

Once more. "R..."

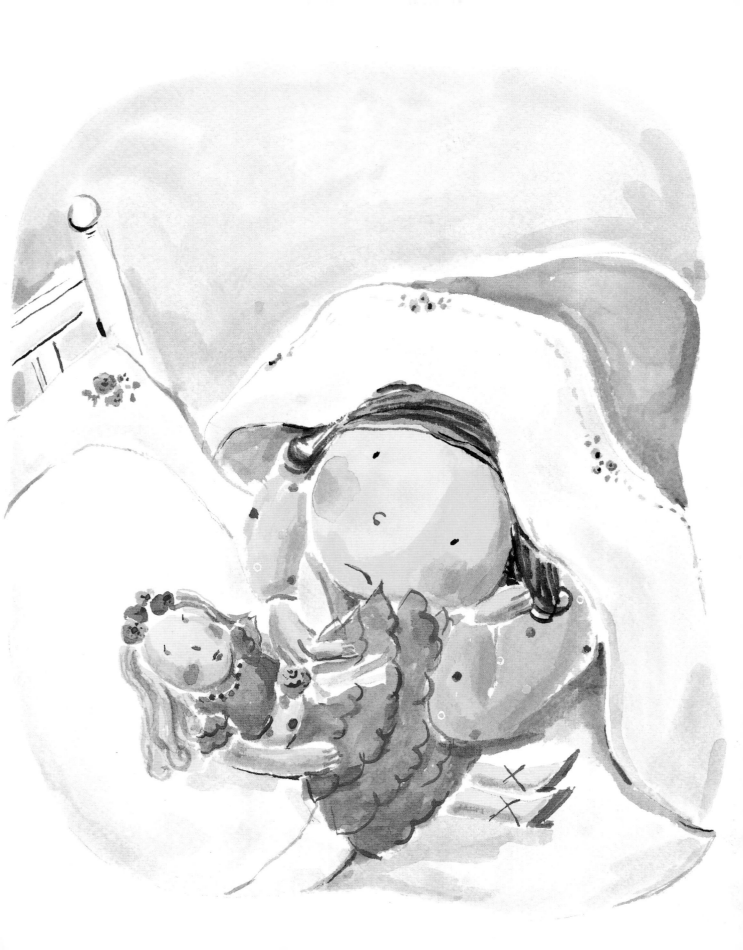

Franny got out of bed.

She put Rose back on the chair.

She straightened Rose's skirt and smoothed her curls.

She was careful not to touch her hand.

Franny felt sad.

Her birthday was over.

The house was quiet, but she was wide-awake.

She couldn't do a puzzle in the dark.

She couldn't play Chinese checkers by herself.

She couldn't catch bugs inside the house.

And Rose could only sing one song.

Franny looked around her room.

There was Suzie, still flopped over on top of the toy shelf.

Franny picked her up.

Suzie was soft the way an old sheet is soft.

She smelled like children.

Franny climbed back into bed.

She and Suzie snuggled down.

Before she fell asleep, Franny squeezed Suzie's soft hand.
Suzie smiled, but she didn't say a word.